Toot & Puddle

Top of the World

by Holly Hobbie

LITTLE, BROWN AND COMPANY
Books for Young Readers
New York   Boston

Little, Brown and Company

Hachette Book Group USA
237 Park Avenue, New York, NY 10017
Visit our Web site at www.lb-kids.com

First Paperback Edition: December 2008
First published in hardcover in 2002 by Little, Brown and Company

Library of Congress Cataloging-in-Publication Data
Hobbie, Holly.
  Toot & Puddle: top of the world / by Holly Hobbie—1st ed.
    p. cm.
Summary: When Toot, a pig who loves to travel, takes a walk that turns into a trip to France and Nepal, his friend Puddle sets out to find him.
    ISBN 978-0-316-36513-0 (hc) / ISBN 978-0-316-03384-8 (pb)
      [1. Pigs—Fiction. 2. Travel—Fiction. 3. Friendship—Fiction. 4. France—Fiction. 5. Nepal—Fiction.] I. Title: Toot and Puddle. II. Title.
PZ7.H6517 Tod 2002
[E]—dc21
2001029450

10 9 8 7 6 5 4 3 2 1

TWP

Printed in Singapore

The illustrations for this book were done in watercolor.
The text was set in Optima, and the display type is Windsor Light.

For Joce and Than

When Puddle came into the kitchen for breakfast,
there was a note on the table.

Puddle cut the grass.

At lunchtime, there was no sign of Toot.
"Maybe he went fishing," Tulip suggested.
"But we always go fishing together," Puddle answered.

Dinnertime came. Toot still wasn't back.
"He never misses dinner," Puddle said.
"This is delicious," said Tulip. "Toot would love it."

"Toot!" Puddle called into the woods.
"Is he lost?" Tulip asked.
"You can't get lost in your own woods," Puddle said.

When it grew dark, Puddle really began to worry.
What if Toot tumbled into a hole and couldn't get out?
Or worse, Puddle thought, *something even worse.*

"I better go search for him," Puddle decided. "He's my best friend."

Puddle walked all through the woods and around Pocket Pond, and he climbed to the top of Orchard Hill searching for his friend. "Toot," he called. "Where are you?"

Ah-ha . . . what do we have here?

Puddle tramped through dark woods until . . .

The starry sky opened before him.
Toot loves trains, he thought.

"AIRPORT!" Puddle said.
Just the other day, Toot was saying he hadn't flown any-
where in months.

Provence, mused Puddle. Now that was one place Toot
had never been.

What am I doing? Puddle asked himself. Now Tulip
would be worried about him, too. But his thought came
too late.

Which way would I go, Puddle wondered, *if I was Toot.*

Yes, Provence was beautiful. But where was his friend?

"Bonjour, mon ami!" Toot cheered.

"Toot!" cried Puddle. "What are you doing here?"

"I guess I got carried away," Toot said. "I hopped onto a train and then a bus and then a plane and then a bicycle. One thing led to another all the way to Coucou Poche. I had a whim," Toot exclaimed. "How in the world did you get here?"

"The same way," Puddle said. "I went looking for you, and one thing just led to another . . . all the way to here."

"That's how whims are," said Toot.

"Isn't it exciting to be in such a faraway place?" Toot asked.

"Tulip will be worried now that we're both missing," said Puddle. "I better give her a jingle."

"I found him," Puddle said. "We're fine. We'll be back soon."

"They have the highest mountain in the world there," Toot said.

"Are you sure this is a good idea?" asked Puddle.

"I'm sure."

"Whew," puffed Puddle, "that was fun."
"I'll say," said Toot.
"I'm glad we did it together," Puddle said.

As they hiked down the mountain, Puddle was quiet.

"What's wrong?" Toot asked. "Are you getting pooped out?"

"I think I'm getting homesick," Puddle admitted.

"That happens to me every time," Toot told him. "I love to go off on a trip, and then when the time comes, I love to get back home."